*Presented to*

..............................................................................................................

*By*

..............................................................................................................

*On*

..........................................................................................

# *My Bible*

Stories and Illustrations by

Chad Frye

A Barbour Book

*My Bible*

ISBN 1-55748-395-7 White
ISBN 1-55748-438-4 Blue
ISBN 1-55748-439-2 Pink



Printed in Belgium

To my Dad

David Frye

Ephesians 6:4

# CONTENTS

## Old Testament Stories

## New Testament Stories

Dear Reader:

Welcome to the world of ***My Bible***, a world just waiting for you.

Do you ever wonder how the world was made? Who is God? Have you ever read about God's Son, Jesus? Do you know how much God and Jesus love you? Will you ever get to meet Jesus? ***My Bible*** will help you answer these questions and many more.

Forty Bible stories—twenty from the Old Testament and twenty from the New Testament—are included. Every word in the Bible, God's special book, is true and every story you'll read really, really happened.

After reading these stories we hope you will want to learn more about the Bible and God's plan for you.

The Publisher

# Old Testament Stories

# ADAM AND EVE

A long, long time ago there was nothing. No earth, no trees, no oceans, no animals, no people! Nothing. But God has always been here, and only God could make the world. God made light, water, earth, plants, the sun, moon, and stars, birds, fish, and animals, and people! The first people were named Adam and Eve. They lived in the Garden of Eden, a perfect place made just for them by God. The Garden of Eden was so wonderful that all creatures lived together happily, even lions and tigers!

***Would you like to live there?***

Genesis 1:1-3:24

# CAIN AND ABEL

○○○○○○○○○

Adam and Eve had to leave the Garden of Eden when they did not obey God. Years later they had two sons. Cain liked to grow things. Abel liked to take care of sheep. One day the brothers decided to make offerings to God as a way of saying thank you. Because God liked offerings of animals, Abel's offering of sheep pleased Him but Cain's fruits and vegetables did not. Cain was so angry that he did a terrible thing: Cain killed Abel. God punished Cain by making him live far away from everyone.

***What should Cain have done?***

Genesis 4:1-16

# Noah and the Flood

○○○○○○○○○

The world had become a very bad place. Only Noah loved God. God told Noah to build an enormous boat, or an ark. The ark would hold Noah's family and two of every kind of animal, plus enough food and water for everyone. Noah's neighbors thought Noah was silly to build such a boat. But as soon as all people and animals were on board, God closed the door of the ark and the rains began. After forty days and nights the earth was entirely under water. Later God made a rainbow in the sky. God promised never again to destroy the earth with water.

***What does it mean to make a promise?***

Genesis 5:32-9:19

# Abraham and Isaac

God surprised Abraham and his wife Sarah. God gave them a baby son, Isaac, when Abraham was 100 years old! When Isaac grew a little older God told Abraham to bring him to the top of a mountain. God wanted Abraham to offer Isaac as an offering...God was asking Abraham to kill his only son! Why would God do that? God wanted to see if Abraham really loved Him. Just when Abraham took out his knife, an angel of God called out to stop him. God loved Abraham, and Abraham loved God.

***How do you think Isaac felt?***

Genesis 22:1-19

# JOSEPH

ooooooooo

Jacob gave his favorite son Joseph a special gift. It was a beautiful coat of many colors! Joseph's brothers became very jealous and they threw Joseph into a pit. Then they sold him to some men who were going to a faraway land. When Jacob saw Joseph's coat, which the brothers had covered with goat's blood, he thought Joseph had been killed by a wild animal. Joseph was taken to Egypt to be a slave, but God had great plans for him. One day Joseph and his brothers would even be friends.

***Do you know what it means to forgive?***

Genesis 37

# God's Laws

○○○○○○○○○

Moses went up to the top of a mountain to talk with God. God wrote some laws on pieces of stone for Moses. These laws told God's special people, the Israelites, how God wanted them to live. The peo-ple of God had forgotten God. When Moses came down from the mountain he saw that the people had made a golden calf to worship instead of God. Moses was so angry that he broke God's stone laws.

***God loves you and wants you to worship only Him. Can you think of three things God wants you to do?***

Exodus 19:17-20; 24; 31:18-32:35; 34

# SAMSON

OOOOOOOOO

Samson was the strongest man in the Bible. Samson's power came from God. One night Samson was in the town of his enemies, the Philistines. Some Philistines found out he was there and locked the gates of the city. This was no problem for Samson. In the middle of the night Samson got up and ripped out the city gates. He put the gates on his shoulders and carried them to the top of a hill almost thirty-eight miles away!

***God has given you a special ability. What things do you like to do?***

Judges 16:1-3

# RUTH AND BOAZ

Ruth had just moved to Bethlehem. Because she was very poor, Ruth went to work in the barley fields of a man named Boaz. Every day she picked up barley that the other workers dropped. Soon Boaz fell in love with Ruth. He told his workers to drop extra barley for Ruth. When Boaz discovered that Ruth loved him too, Boaz went to the leaders of the town. He told them that he wanted to marry Ruth. Many months later God gave Ruth and Boaz a baby boy named Obed.

***Do you know that you too are a gift from God?***

The Book of Ruth

# HANNAH

OOOOOOOO

Year after year Hannah came to the temple to pray for a baby. But this year was different. Hannah was praying, crying, and moving her mouth without speaking all at the same time! Eli the priest told Hannah that God would answer her prayers. Several months later God gave Hannah and her husband a baby son, Samuel. A few years later Samuel came back to the temple to live with Eli. Every year Hannah brought Samuel a new coat she had made for him. One day Samuel would be a prophet, an important man of God.

***When something bothers you, do you tell God?***

1 Samuel 1: 1 - 2:21

# David the Shepherd

ooooooooo

David the shepherd boy was Obed's grandson, and Ruth's great-grandson. He loved to sing songs about God and play his harp as he sat in the fields watching the sheep. He also practiced using his sling. He was a good shot. Watching sheep was a big job for David. One day a lion tried to trap one of David's lambs. With God's help, David quickly killed the lion. Another time God helped David overcome a bear. Later, David would use his sling when he came face to face with Goliath, a giant nine feet tall!

***Why was David so brave?***

1 Samuel 17:34-37

# Solomon's Temple

OOOOOOOOO

Many years later David became king. King David wanted to build a temple for God but God told him no. David was a king of war and he had to protect Israel. David's son, Solomon, was a king of peace. King Solomon would build the temple. Building the temple was a big job, but Solomon did it with God's help. The temple was made of big stones and cedar trees. Solomon put many golden statues and fancy brass objects in the temple. After seven years the temple was finished.

***Can you take some clay and make your own temple to God?***

1 Kings 5-8

# Naboth's Vineyard

Many years after King Solomon died, Ahab became king of Israel. One day King Ahab went to visit a man named Naboth. Naboth had a vineyard where he grew big juicy grapes, and Ahab wanted that vineyard. Naboth would not sell or trade his land because his family had owned the vineyard for a long time. Queen Jezebel saw that the king was unhappy and she did something very bad. She told some men to kill Naboth so that King Ahab could have the vineyard. One day God would punish Ahab and Jezebel.

***How can you remember to be kind to others?***

1 Kings 7: 21

NABOTH'S
VINEYARD

# Elijah's Contest

○○○○○○○○○

Elijah wanted his people to love the one true God, and not a fake god named Baal. A contest was held between Elijah and Baal's prophets. Only the true god would send fire from the sky to burn the animal sacrifices. Baal's prophets yelled and jumped around to get Baal to notice them. No fire came. Elijah had twelve barrels of water poured on his sacrifice, and then he prayed. God sent a fire so hot that it burned up the bull, wood, stones, water, and the dust on the ground!

***What does this story tell you about God?***

1 Kings 18:17-40

# LITTLE KING JOSIAH

OOOOOOOOO

How old do you have to be to become a king? Josiah became king when he was only eight years old! His father had been a bad king who had worshiped idols and not the one true God. Josiah chose to serve only God. He ordered that all the idols in the country be destroyed and he began to repair God's temple. Hidden under old stones was the book of the law of the Lord, given to God's people by Moses. King Josiah read God's Word and he and his country obeyed God.

***Was Josiah a good king?***

2 Kings 22-23:30;
2 Chronicles 34-35

# NEHEMIAH

○○○○○○○○○

When Israel was once attacked, many people were taken away to another land to be slaves, including Nehemiah. Nehemiah became a cupbearer for a king. Back in Israel the walls of the biggest city had crumbled. Nehemiah asked the king if he could go back home to build the walls again. The king agreed and he even gave Nehemiah some wood to make new gates. Working on the walls, Nehemiah and his men kept their swords ready, but God protected Israel and the walls were rebuilt in only fifty-two days.

***When others ask you to help, what do you say?***

Nehemiah 1:1-7:4

# Queen Esther

○○○○○○○○○

Esther was so beautiful that King Ahasuerus chose her to be his queen. In the king's court there was also a man named Haman. Haman hated the Jews, especially a man named Mordecai. No one in the palace knew that Mordecai was Esther's cousin and that Esther herself was a Jew! When Esther found out that Haman intended to kill all the Jews, she invited the king and Haman to two big parties. At the second party the king asked Esther if she wanted anything. This was Esther's chance! Esther saved her cousin and her people, the Jews.

***Why does God want us to love each other?***

The Book of Esther

# Job

OOOOOOOO

Job loved God very much. Satan, the devil, thought Job loved God because he was rich. To prove Job's goodness, God let Satan do terrible things to Job and his family. But God would not let Satan kill Job. Job's animals were stolen, fire fell from the sky on his servants and sheep, Job lost his family, and ugly sores covered Job's body. Job was very upset, but he did not say bad things about God. God was so happy that He gave Job ten more children and twice as many things as he had before.

***How can you make God happy?***

The Book of Job

# JEREMIAH

OOOOOOOO

Jeremiah was another prophet of God. The people of Israel did not obey God and Jeremiah felt very sad. God was going to punish them. Jeremiah told some princes that God was going to let another country, Babylon, capture Israel. The princes did not like to hear such bad news. They threw Jeremiah into a deep dungeon that was filled with slime. One kind man heard Jeremiah's cries. He made a rope out of old cloths but Jeremiah was so stuck in the slime that it took thirty men to pull him out.

***How is God like your mom and dad?***

Jeremiah 38

# The Fiery Furnace

○○○○○○○○○

Once King Nebuchadnezzar made a great statue of gold. Anyone who would not bow down to the statue would be thrown into a very hot furnace. Three men—Shadrach, Meshach, and Abednego—would not bow down. Because they loved God more than any statue, the king had them thrown into the leaping flames. But God sent an angel to protect Shadrach, Meshach, and Abednego. They were able to walk around in the fire without getting hurt!

***God doesn't want you to play with fire, but He does want you to love Him. How can you do that?***

Daniel 3

# Daniel and the Lions

○○○○○○○○○

King Darius felt terrible! He had signed a law—which couldn't be broken—and now his most trusted friend, Daniel, was about to be thrown into a den full of sharp-toothed, starving lions! The law said that everyone must ask King Darius for anything they wanted. Daniel loved God and he refused to ask the king if he could pray. King Darius knew at this moment Daniel was probably only bones. The next morning the king raced to the den. Daniel was alive and well! God had protected Daniel.

***Do you have to be afraid if you love God?***

Daniel 6

# New Testament Stories

# Mary

○○○○○○○○○

God sent the angel Gabriel to give a message to Mary. Mary was a young woman from the town of Nazareth who loved God. She was going to marry Joseph, a man who built things out of wood. God had chosen Mary to be the mother of a most wonderful baby, and that baby's name would be Jesus. Gabriel told her that the Holy Spirit —God's Spirit—would perform a miracle. Jesus would be born in a human body, but He would be God's perfect Son.

***Can you think of a happy day you have had?***

Luke 1:26-38

# Jesus Is Born

When it was almost time for Jesus to be born, Mary and Joseph had to travel to Bethlehem. It was a long trip. When they got there, there was no room anywhere for them, so they stayed in a stable with some animals. That night Mary had her special baby right there in the stable. Jesus' first little bed was a manger from which animals ate their food. Nearby, an angel told some shepherds that Jesus had been born. The sky was filled with angels singing to God.

***How would you feel if you were a shepherd on that night?***

Luke 2:1-21

# The Wise Men

○○○○○○○○○

The night Jesus was born a special star shone above the little stable. From far away some wise men saw the star and knew somehow that a king—Jesus—had been born. The wise men asked King Herod if he knew where a baby king had been born. King Herod did not know about Jesus, but he did not want another king. The wise men followed the star and found Jesus. They bowed down before Jesus and gave Him beautiful gifts, the gifts a king should have.

***Do you know Jesus is still our king?***

Matthew 2:1-12

# Jesus in the Temple

○○○○○○○○○

When Jesus was older He went to the temple, God's special place for worship. Some people had set up tables in the temple where they were selling birds to give as offerings to God. Jesus was so angry that he pushed all the tables over, spilling the money everywhere. He told the people that the temple was to be used for prayer and not for making money. Later many sick people came to Jesus in the temple. Jesus made them well again. Jesus knew that He was doing what God wanted Him to do.

***What should you do in church?***

Matthew 21:12-17; Mark 11:15-19

# ZACCHAEUS

OOOOOOOOO

Nobody liked Zacchaeus. He made people pay more money than they should for taxes and then he kept it for himself! One day a big crowd was waiting to see Jesus. Because Zacchaeus was small, he climbed up a tree for a better view. Jesus stopped under the tree and looked up. Jesus said, "Zacchaeus, come down. I am going to your house." Happily, Zacchaeus climbed down. Jesus cared about Zacchaeus! Later that day Zacchaeus promised to give half of his money to the poor and return the money he had stolen.

***Why did Zacchaeus give back the money?***

Luke 19:1-10

# The Pool at Bethesda

OOOOOOOOO

In the city of Jerusalem, near a sheep market, there was a pool of water known as Bethesda. Many sick and handicapped people liked to be at this pool. They believed they could be made well at certain times by the rising and bubbling water. One day Jesus was visiting the pool. He noticed a man lying on a mat. Jesus knew this man had not walked for thirty-eight years. Jesus said, "Rise, pick up your mat, and walk." The man did just that! Jesus, the Son of God, had healed him.

***Does Jesus know when you are sick?***

John 5:2-18

# Peter Feels Bad

ooooooooo

Peter once told Jesus that he would give his life for Him. Jesus said, "Tonight, before the rooster crows, you will say three times that you do not know Me." Later that night Jesus was arrested. Peter waited outside the house where Jesus was taken. A girl nearby said that Peter was one of Jesus' followers. Peter said, "I do not know Him." Another person also said that Peter was Jesus' friend. Peter said, "I am not!" A third person also recognized Peter. Peter said, "I don't know what you are talking about!" The rooster crowed. Peter walked away and cried.

***Why was Peter sad?***

Matthew 26:31-35, 69-75; Mark 14:27-31, 66-72; Luke 22:31-34, 54-62; John 13:36-38, 18:25-27

# Jesus Is Judged

○○○○○○○○○

One of the men to judge Jesus was named Pontius Pilate. Pilate said Jesus had not done anything wrong. Another governor said the same thing. Pilate told an angry crowd that he would let Jesus go free. The people shouted, "No! Release Barabbas instead!" Barabbas, a man who had killed someone, was freed, while Jesus was sent to die on the cross. For three years Jesus had been telling others about the love of God. Many followed Him, but it was God's plan that Jesus should die.

***Find out why by turning the page.***

Matthew 27:11-26; Luke 22:66-23:25

# Jesus Dies for Us

Angry people shouted at Jesus as He walked to the cross. A crown of ugly, sharp thorns was put on His head. Soldiers were ordered to nail Jesus to the cross. At noon that day the sky became dark for three whole hours. In great pain, Jesus finally cried, "Father, forgive them!" Then He died. A soldier said, "This really was the Son of God." Jesus, who had done nothing wrong, died because He loved the world. Because Jesus died, anyone who believes in Him will someday live forever with Him in heaven.

***How do you know Jesus loves you?***

Matthew 27:27-56; Mark 15:16-41;
Luke 23:26-49; John 19:17-37

# Jesus Is Alive!

OOOOOOOO

Jesus—the Son of God—had said He would die but then He would be alive three days later. Some of Jesus' enemies made sure soldiers were watching the place, or the tomb, where Jesus was buried. They did not want Jesus' friends to steal his body and say Jesus was really alive. Three days after Jesus died two women went to the tomb and saw that the gigantic stone in front of the opening had been rolled away. Two angels were sitting where Jesus' body had been. Jesus had risen from the dead, just as He said!

***Why is Jesus so special?***

Matthew 27:57-28:10; Mark 15:42-16:14;
Luke 23:50-24:12; John 19:38-20:18

# STEPHEN

○○○○○○○○○

Stephen loved to share the good news of Jesus. But some people who did not believe in Jesus did not like what Stephen said. They lied about Stephen to get him into trouble. They said that Stephen was saying bad things about Moses and God that he never really said. The people grabbed him, took him out of the city, and threw stones at him until he died. Even though they hated him, Stephen prayed for them.

***When you love Jesus, you don't hate anyone, even those who hurt you. Can you remember that?***

Acts 6:3-15, 7:54-8:3

# A Chariot from Ethiopia

OOOOOOOOO

Philip, a follower of Jesus, was told by an angel of God to walk toward the city of Gaza. On his way he met an important man from Ethiopia riding in a chariot, reading the Bible. The man invited him inside the chariot and Philip shared his love of God's Word. As they passed some water, the man ordered the chariot to stop and he was baptized by Philip. As Philip came up out of the water, God suddenly took him to a city twenty miles away!

***Have you ever seen someone baptized?***

Acts 8:26-40

# SAUL OF TARSUS

○○○○○○○○○

Saul's job was to find Jesus' followers, or Christians, and have them killed. But God had a different plan for Saul. As Saul was on his way to Damascus, he was blinded by a light from heaven. That day his whole life was changed. Now he would share the love of Jesus. Now he would be called Paul. Some people in Damascus did not like to hear Paul talk about Jesus and they planned to hurt him. Paul was lowered down the city wall in a basket. Paul's adventures for Jesus had just begun!

***How are you like Paul?***

Acts 9:1-31

# Dorcas

ooooooooo

Dorcas liked doing special things for other people, especially sewing beautiful robes for them to wear. One day, however, Dorcas became very sick and died. Dorcas's friends learned that Peter was nearby and they asked him to come. Peter went to the room where Dorcas's body lay. He asked to be left alone because he wanted to pray. Then Peter said, "Dorcas, arise." Dorcas sat up, alive! God had given Peter the power to bring Dorcas back to life.

***If you saw this happen, what would you do? Would you tell someone about Jesus?***

Acts 9:36-43

# Peter Is Set Free

○○○○○○○○○

King Herod, the grandson of the Herod who ruled when Jesus was born, had captured Peter and was going to kill him. Peter's friends stayed up all night, every night, praying for him. One night an angel woke Peter in prison. Peter's chains fell off as the angel told him to put on his shoes and coat. The angel led Peter out of the jail and into the street and then disappeared. When Peter's friends saw that he had been set free, they thought they were seeing his ghost!

***Do you pray to God every day?***

Acts 12:1-19

# LYDIA

OOOOOOOO

Lydia sold purple dye that was used to make purple clothes. Lydia loved God. Often she would pray with other women by the river. One day Lydia met Paul and his friend Silas. Paul had become a missionary, or a person who travels great distances telling others about Jesus. The day Lydia met Paul was the first time she had heard the good news about Jesus! Lydia invited Paul and Silas to stay in her home while they were in Philippi.

***Have you become friends with Jesus?***

Acts 16:11-40

# MARS' HILL

○○○○○○○○○

Paul was in Athens, Greece. He walked around the city and saw that everyone worshiped many idols. They even worshiped an idol "To the Unknown God," in case there was a god they did not know about. Paul began to tell the people about Jesus. The people took Paul to a place called Mars' Hill where he told them about the one real God, the god they did not know about. Some people made fun of him, some people wanted to hear more, and some believed in God.

***Can someone help you find Greece on a map or globe?***

Acts 17:15-34

# Paul's Guards

OOOOOOOOO

Paul was in jail again because he loved to talk about Jesus. This time more than forty Jews promised they would not eat or drink until they had killed Paul. Paul's nephew overheard them talking and he told Paul about them. In the middle of the night 200 soldiers, 70 soldiers on horses, and 200 soldiers with spears all took Paul to another town. Imagine how hungry those forty men must have been! God would not let them kill Paul.

***Today we can talk about Jesus and not go to jail. Can you tell someone that Jesus loves them?***

Acts 23:11-35

# Shipwrecked!

○○○○○○○○○

Paul was sailing for Rome aboard a prison ship. Paul was going to see Caesar, the ruler of all Rome. Suddenly a strong wind started to blow. Big, crashing waves tossed the ship around for days. When the ship broke apart, everyone jumped into the water and swam to an island. God had told Paul that everyone on board would live. Paul told the people on the island about Jesus and even healed those who were sick. God saved Paul from the storm, and now Paul brought others to God.

***Do you know that God has a plan for you?***

Acts 27:1-28:11

# We Will See Jesus Again

○○○○○○○○

Jesus promised He will return to earth. Someday—we do not know when—Jesus will meet us in the sky. There will be a loud shout and a trumpet will be heard. Then, faster than you can blink your eye, everyone who believes in Jesus will fly up into the air to meet Him. Even Christians who have died will meet Jesus. As Christians, we should not be afraid to die because we know we will live in heaven someday with Jesus.

***Do you believe in Jesus? You can invite Jesus to come into your heart right now.***

John 14:1-3; 1 Corinthians 15:51-58;
1 Thessalonians 4:13-18

MARTINDALE
I Cor. 15:52

Chad Frye is the author of two other books for children. His first book, ***The Fun Bible Search Book. . .Find Rupert*** is a best-selling children's title.

Chad lives in Spartanburg, South Carolina.